THE SNOWMAIDEN

Copyright © Text James Riordan 1990
Copyright © Illustrations Stephen Lambert 1990

First published in Great Britain in 1990
by Hutchinson Children's Books
An imprint of The Random Century Group
20 Vauxhall Bridge Road
London SW1V 2SA

Random Century Australia (Pty) Ltd
20 Alfred Street, Milsons Point, Sydney, NSW 2061

Random Century New Zealand Limited
32-34 View Road, PO Box 40-086, Glenfield, Auckland 10

Century Hutchinson South Africa (Pty) Ltd
PO Box 337, Bergvlei 2012, South Africa

Printed and bound in Hong Kong
Designed by Philippa Bramson

British Library Cataloguing in Publication Data
Riordan, James, 1936
The snowmaiden.
I. Russian tales. Texts. For Children.
I. Title.
398.2'1'0947

ISBN 0-09-173861-X

THE SNOWMAIDEN

RETOLD BY JAMES RIORDAN

ILLUSTRATED BY STEPHEN LAMBERT

HUTCHINSON

LONDON SYDNEY AUCKLAND JOHANNESBURG

IT was midnight. The full moon cast a silver glow upon the wintry scene. Suddenly, the sky was full of birds returning from warmer lands and Spring in all her glory came floating down to earth on the back of a swan.

'What a cold, uncheery welcome greets us here,' she said. 'Winter has put the dancing brooks in chains, the meadows lie barren, the trees are silent and bare.'

As she spoke, the birds around her shivered in the chill night air. Spring trembled too from cold and shame.

'I am the cause of your suffering,' she lamented. 'Sixteen years ago I flirted with old red-nosed Frost. Since then he has held our daughter, Snowmaiden, in his power and we must endure this long, cruel winter.'

SPRING sighed, thinking of her daughter whom she loved
dearly. At that moment, the giant figure of red-nosed Frost
strode out from the trees.

'Greetings, fair Spring,' he said.

'How is our daughter, Snowmaiden?' she asked.

'She is well. I keep her safe within my icy forest realm.'

'You know nothing of a maiden's heart,' said Spring, crossly.
'She is sixteen and needs freedom to go wherever she chooses.'

'But what if Yarilo, the sun god should see her?' old Frost
replied. 'He would melt her clean away!'

Snowmaiden's parents argued deep into the night until they
finally agreed to put her in the care of a childless peasant couple.

NEXT morning, two old peasants were out walking in the forest gathering brushwood for their stove. The old man was in good spirits, singing loudly. His wife was not so happy: the sound of children's laughter from the village pierced her heart, reminding her that she had no child of her own.

'Cheer up, old girl,' said her husband. 'I tell you what, let's make a daughter out of snow.'

The old woman grew angry at his foolishness. But he ignored her grumbles and set to gathering piles of snow. First he rolled a snowball, then added arms and legs and finally placed a snow head on snow shoulders. He stuck on a nose and drew a mouth and eyes.

NEXT something happened that made the old pair gasp. The snowmaiden's lips grew red, her eyes opened wide; she gazed fondly at the old pair and smiled a warm, grateful smile. Then, shaking off the snowflakes, she stepped out of the snow – a real, live girl!

The old man stood back, amazed. He fancied the light was playing tricks with his eyes; yet his wife was staring too. At last he found his tongue, 'What is your name?' he asked.

'I am Snowmaiden,' was all she said.

Without more ado they led her to their cottage.

IN the passing of time, Snowmaiden grew up not by the day, but by the hour; and every day she seemed more lovely than before. Her skin was whiter than the driven snow; her fair hair gleamed with a touch of ash or silver birch; her eyes were bluer than the frosty sapphire sky.

There was no end to the old pair's love for their daughter and they doted on her every minute of the day. She grew up modest and kind. And when she lifted up her voice to sing, the whole village stopped to listen.

Soon, spring sunshine arrived to warm the land. Patches of green grass appeared amid the snowy wastes, and larks took up their woodland song.

YET with the coming of warmer days, Snowmaiden grew sad. She would hide from the sun, seek a chill shadow and stretch out her pale arms to the rain. Once, a black storm cloud burst, showering the village with hailstones as big as buttons. She ran out to catch the hail as though it were precious gems. But no sooner had the sun melted the hail than she burst into tears so bitter you would have thought a sister was mourning for her own dear brother.

ONE day, as summer was approaching, a group of village girls called on Snowmaiden to invite her out to play. But Snowmaiden shrank back into the shadows.

'Go on, daughter,' the old woman urged, 'go out and enjoy yourself in the sunshine.'

A village girl took Snowmaiden by the hand and led her from the cottage. The other girls were happy, they gathered flowers, plaited them into garlands, sang songs and skipped along the forest paths. A band of young men joined the girls and soon the whole village was alive with merrymaking.

ONLY Snowmaiden was sad. She walked alone, no smile upon her frozen lips. Then all of a sudden she heard the lilting music of a flute; she glanced up and saw a humble shepherd boy standing before her.

'Dear Snowmaiden, come and join the dance,' he said. 'I'll play my flute for you alone.'

Lel the shepherd boy was drawn to this lovely, gentle maid and kindly took her by the hand. Everyone looked on in wonder as Snowmaiden whirled round and round with her merry partner. Slowly a pink flush of joy appeared upon her pallid cheeks.

FROM that day forth, Lel would often come to play his flute beneath her window, inviting her to walk with him through fields and meadows. Willingly, the maiden ran out to greet her friend. But though he grew to love her dearly, Lel felt no answering warmth within her heart.

ONE day, Lel was walking alone when the beautiful dark-eyed Anna came in sight. Now Anna had grown jealous of Lel's fondness for Snowmaiden and, seeing him alone, she cried, 'How glad I am to find you, Lel. My heart is yours, if you would but take it.'

Just at that moment, Snowmaiden emerged from the trees and chanced upon the pair. At once, Lel broke away and ran to her. 'Dearest Snowmaiden,' he gently said, 'Anna's heart is warm, like mine. But yours is cold and empty.'

Tears fell on pale cheeks and Snowmaiden turned and fled into the forest depths.

SHE did not stop until she came to a deep lake mantled by pink-white lilies. Standing on the bank, she cried out, 'Mother, in grief and anguish your daughter calls to you. I want to love. Give me a human heart, I beg of you.'

Out of the lake rose fair Spring and gazed fondly at her sobbing child.

'Have you forgotten your father's warning?' her mother said. 'You know you cannot be as other girls.'

'If that be so I'd sooner die,' said Snowmaiden. 'To love for a moment, however brief, is dearer to me than a frozen heart.'

Fair Spring sighed. 'The source of love lies in the crown upon my head. Take it and put it on.'

Joyfully, Snowmaiden took the crown of lilies and placed it on her own fair head. At once she shouted out, 'What strange feeling beats within my breast? My eyes are opening to the beauty of the world; my ears can hear the birds' song, my heart is full of the joy of spring.'

'Child,' her mother said, 'you will soon know the power of love within your heart. But heed my words: guard your love from Yarilo's fiery gaze. Do not linger in the crimson rays of dawn; run swiftly to seek the leafy shade and coolness of the wood.'

With those last words, Spring sank below the glistening waters.

SNOWMAIDEN skipped along the woodland paths. Her heart beat faster as she caught the clear notes of a flute. Rushing towards the sound, she soon came to a sunny woodland glade. There Lel the shepherd sat. On seeing his Snowmaiden he jumped up and cried out with joy, 'Snowmaiden, I have looked for you the whole day long. Forgive my hasty words, you must be angry.'

'It is not anger that fills my heart,' she softly replied. 'It is love. Now I know there is no deeper feeling in the world.'

'So you do have a heart, Snowmaiden,' said Lel, joyfully.

At that moment Snowmaiden glanced up at the sky. 'We must hurry,' she said. 'Yarilo's rays already frighten me. Come with me. I must find shade or they will cause me pain.'

'Dear Snowmaiden,' replied Lel, 'we cannot hide our love forever from the light of day.'

As he was speaking, the radiant sun rose higher in the cloudless sky, dispelling the mists of dawn and melting the last trace of snow.

A ray of sunshine fell on Snowmaiden. With a cry of pain she tore herself away and begged Lel to play for her one last time.

Putting the flute to his lips, he began to play a haunting tune. As she listened, tears rolled down her cheeks, colour drained from her lovely face, and her feet began to melt away beneath her.

SLOWLY, her body sank into the damp grey earth, until all that remained was the crown of lilies. A wisp of white mist rose up and vanished into the cloudless sky.

'Dear Snowmaiden,' cried Lel, 'you begged me to protect you from the sun, but I would not listen. Now you have gone like the last spring snows.'

But no one heard his cry. No one, that is, except a grieving mother in a lily-mantled lake, and old red-nosed Frost far away in the northern snows.

Yet as one life passed, another was born. Sunshine awoke the cold earth with a kiss, and brought forth rue and celandine, juniper and cranberry, bird cherry and lilac blossom.

As for Lel, he would wait until the winter snows once more returned to him his Snowmaiden.